SCHOLASTIC News

Nonfiction Readers

Uranus

by
Christine Taylor-Butler

Children's Press®
A Division of Scholastic Inc.
New York Toronto London Auckland Sydney
Mexico City New Delhi Hong Kong
Danbury, Connecticut

These content vocabulary word builders
are for grades 1-2.

Consultants: Daniel D. Kelson, Ph.D.
Carnegie Observatories
Pasadena, CA
and
Andrew Fraknoi
Astronomy Department, Foothill College

Photo Credits:

Photographs © 2005: AP/Wide World Photos: cover; Getty Images/Antonio M. Rosario/The Image Bank: 5 top left, 9; NASA: back cover, 1, 2, 4 top, 4 bottom right, 5 bottom, 7, 13, 15, 17, 19, 23 right; Photo Researchers, NY/Detlev van Ravenswaay: 4 bottom left; PhotoDisc/Getty Images via SODA: 23 left. Illustration on page 5 and 11 by Pat Rasch Diagram on pages 20-21 by Greg Harris

Book Design: Simonsays Design!

Library of Congress Cataloging-in-Publication Data

Taylor-Butler, Christine.
  Uranus / by Christine Taylor-Butler.
    p. cm. — (Scholastic news nonfiction readers)
  Includes bibliographical references and index.
  ISBN 0-516-24915-0 (lib. bdg.)
  1. Uranus (Planet)—Juvenile literature. I. Title. II. Series.
  QB681.T39 2005
  523.47—dc22

                         2005003633

1 2 3 4 5 6 7 8 9 10 R 14 13 12 11 10 09 08 07 06 05

CONTENTS

WORD HUNT

Look for these words as you read. They will be in **bold**.

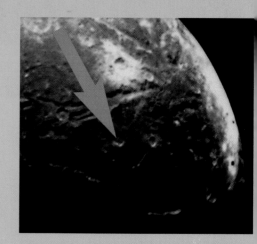

crater
(**kray**-tur)

solar system
(**soh**-lur **siss**-tuhm)

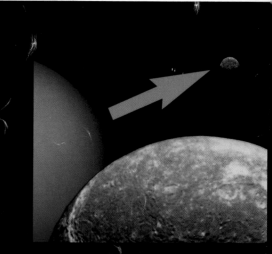

Titania
(tuh-**tane**-yuh)

gas giants
(gass **jye**-uhnts)

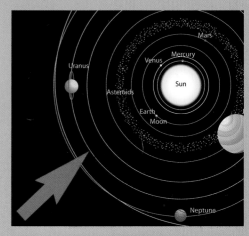

orbit
(**or**-bit)

Uranus
(**yur**-uh-nus)

Voyager 2
(**voi**-ij-uhr 2)

Uranus!

Uranus has an ocean.

Can you swim in the ocean on Uranus?

No, you cannot.

The ocean on Uranus is gas that changed into liquid.

It is very hot.

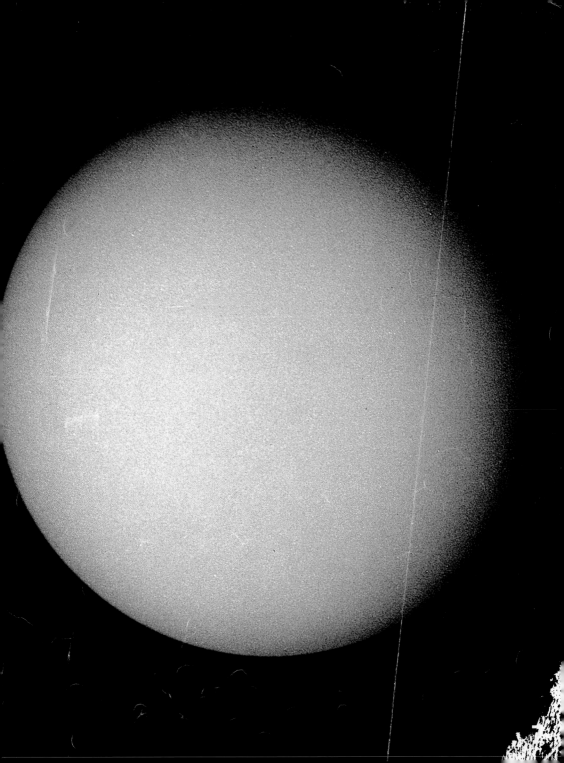

Uranus is the seventh planet from the Sun.

Uranus, Jupiter, Neptune, and Saturn are the biggest planets in our **solar system**.

Sometimes they are called the **gas giants**.

They are mostly made of gas.

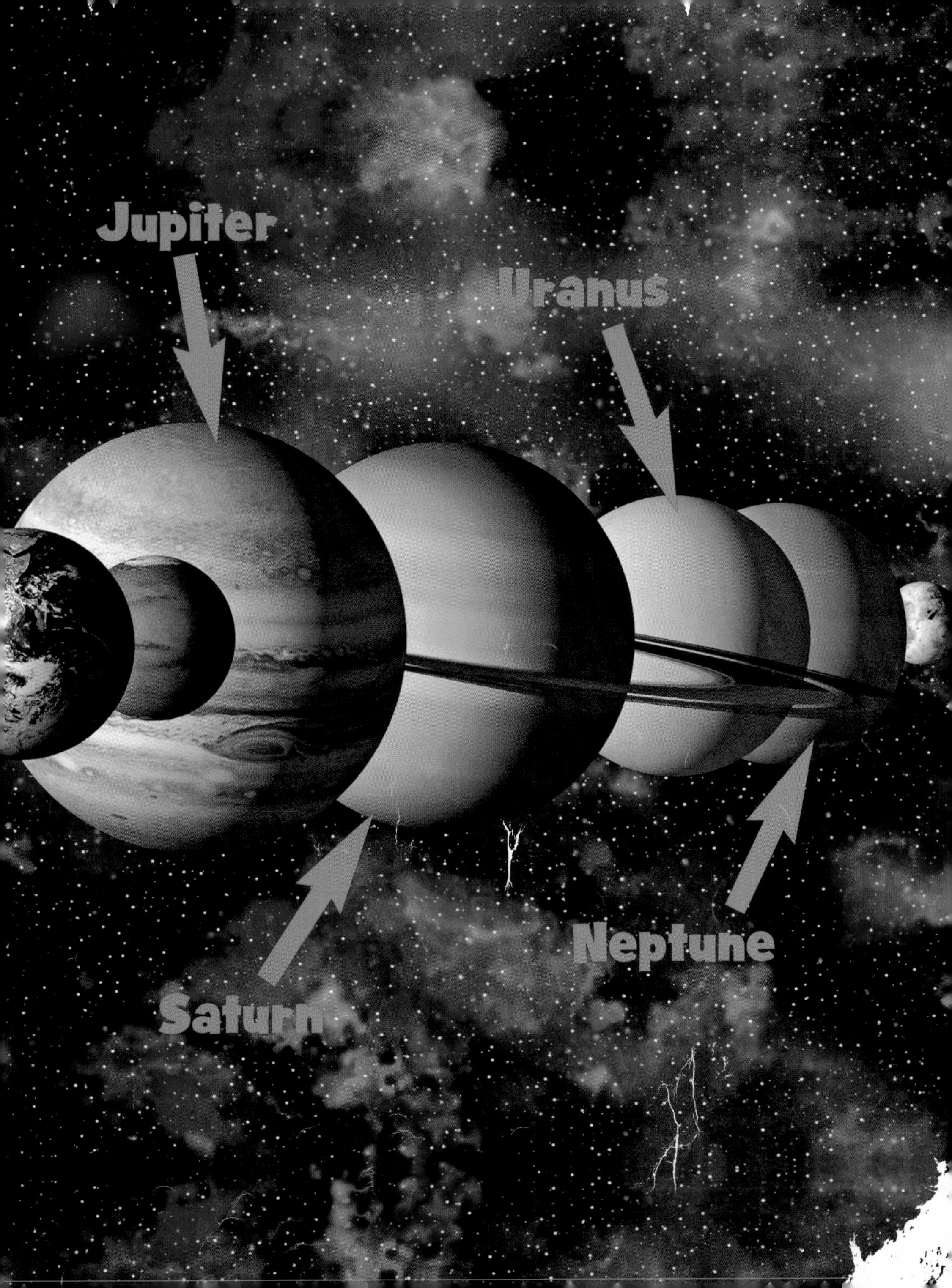
Jupiter
Uranus
Saturn
Neptune

Uranus **orbits** the Sun on its side.

It spins like a wheel.

The other planets in our solar system spin like tops.

Scientists think Uranus was hit by something that tipped it sideways.

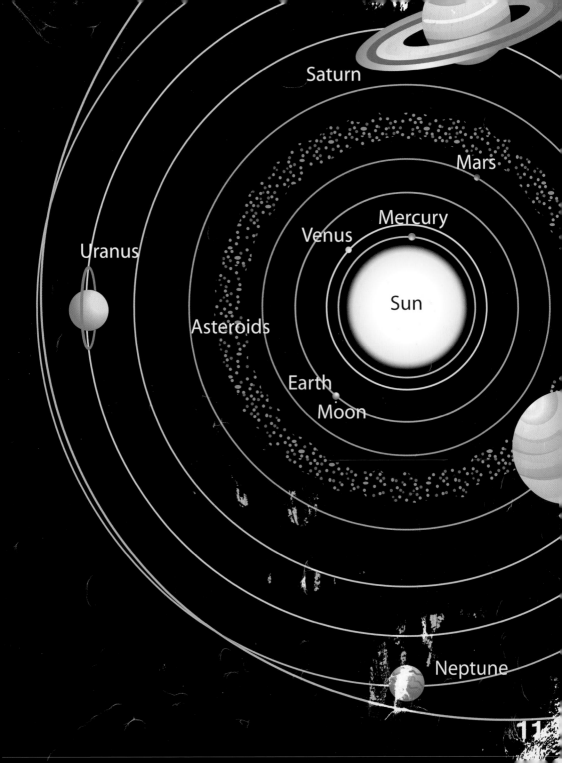

Saturn

Mars

Mercury

Venus

Uranus

Sun

Asteroids

Earth

Moon

Neptune

Uranus has 11 rings.

They are hard to see.

The rings on Uranus are made of ice. The ice is covered in dark dust.

Uranus has more than 27 moons.

The largest moon is **Titania**.

Titania has **craters**, like Earth's moon.

It also has long, deep marks that stretch around it.

Uranus and 5 of its moons.

Miranda is also one of Uranus's moons.

Miranda is one of the oddest worlds anywhere.

It has craters. It has long marks. It has broken rocks. It has giant cliffs.

Scientists know how Miranda got some marks but they do not know about them all.

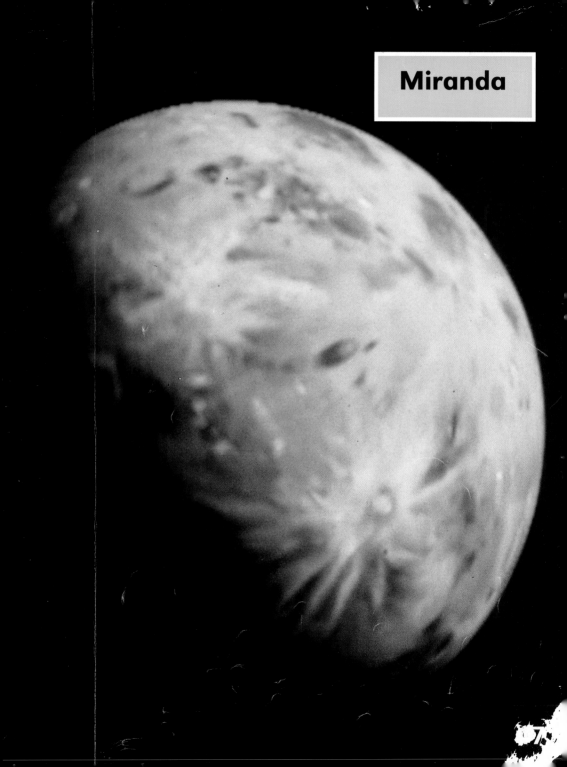

Miranda

Voyager 2 is a space probe.

It is the only craft to go near Uranus.

It is why we know more about this planet.

Thank you, *Voyager 2*!

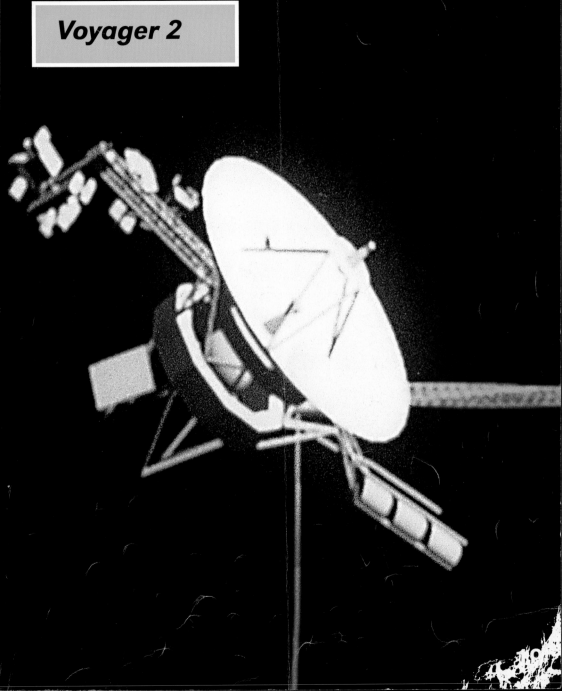

Voyager 2

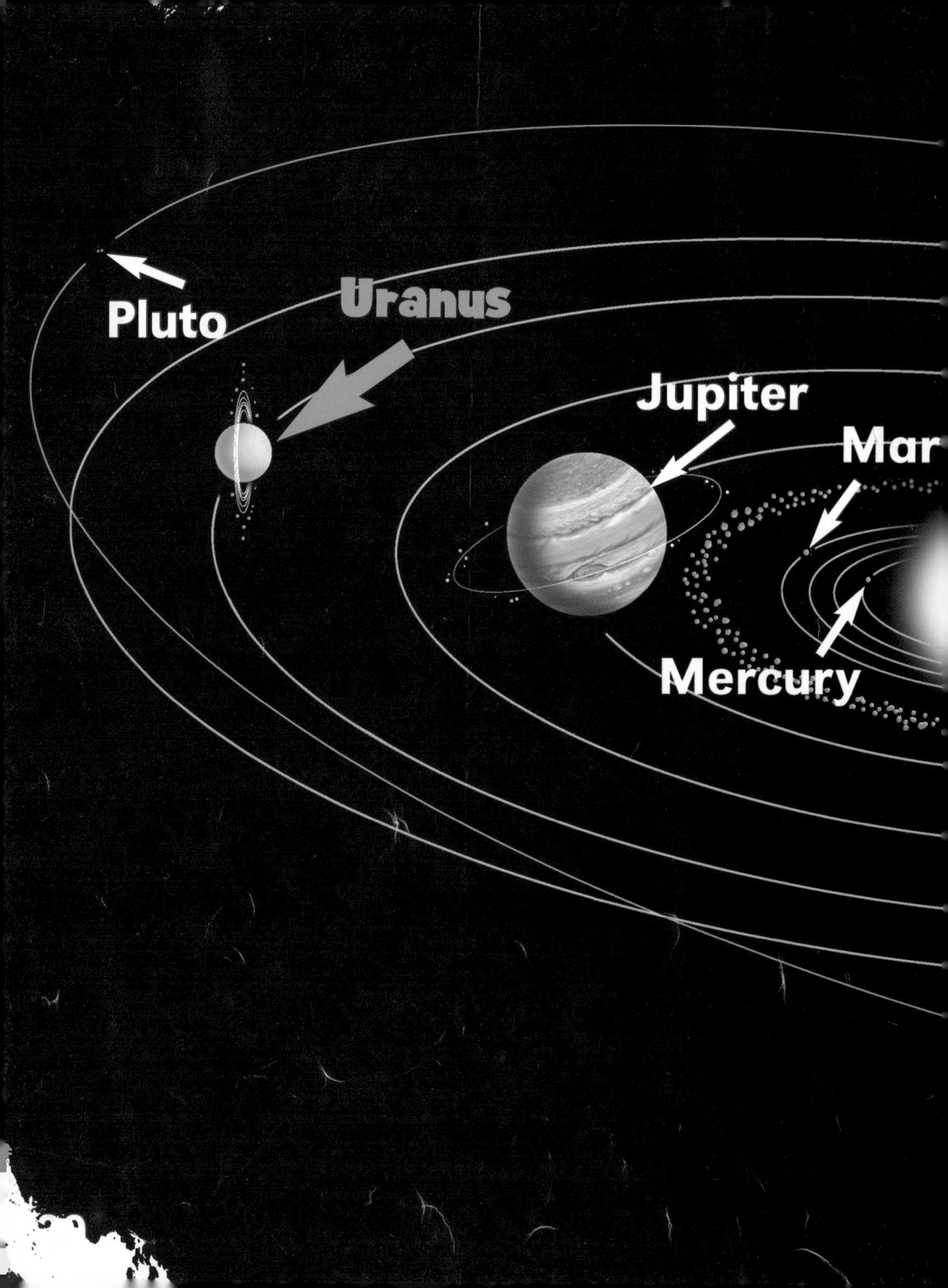
Pluto
Uranus
Jupiter
Mar
Mercury

URANUS

IN OUR SOLAR SYSTEM

Sun

Venus

Saturn

Earth

Neptune

YOUR NEW WORDS

crater (**kray**-tur) a large hole in the ground made by a comet or meteorite

gas giants (gass **jye**-uhnts) the four largest planets

orbit (**or**-bit) the path around an object

solar system (**soh**-lur **siss**-tuhm) the group of planets, moons, and other things that travel around the Sun

Titania (tuh-**tane**-yuh) Uranus's largest moon

Uranus (**yur**-uh-nus) a planet named after the Roman god of the sky

Voyager 2 (**voi**-ij-uhr 2) the first and only space probe to visit Uranus and Neptune

Earth and Uranus

A year is how long it takes a planet to go around the Sun.

 Earth's year =365 days

 Uranus's year =30,687 Earth days

A day is how long it takes a planet turn one time.

 Earth's day = 24 hours

 Uranus's day = 17 Earth hours

A moon is an object that circles around a planet.

 Earth has 1 moon

 Uranus has at least 27 moons

Did you know scientists do not know which way is North on Uranus?

INDEX

FIND OUT MORE

Book:
Children's Atlas of the Universe
By Robert Burnham
Reader's Digest Children's Publishing, Inc., 2000

Website:
Solar System Exploration
http://sse.jpl.nasa.gov/planets

MEET THE AUTHOR:

Christine Taylor-Butler is the author of more than 20 books for children. She holds a degree in Engineering from M.I.T. She lives in Kansas City with her family, where they have a telescope for searching the skies.